HORSES
of
MYTH

HORSES
—OF—
Myth

Gerald and Loretta Hausman
PICTURES BY ROBERT FLORCZAK

DUTTON CHILDREN'S BOOKS · NEW YORK

DUTTON CHILDREN'S BOOKS
A division of Penguin Young Readers Group

Published by the Penguin Group
Penguin Group (USA) Inc., 375 Hudson Street, New York, New York 10014, U.S.A. · Penguin Group (Canada),
10 Alcorn Avenue, Toronto, Ontario, Canada M4V 3B2 (a division of Pearson Penguin Canada Inc.) ·
Penguin Books Ltd, 80 Strand, London WC2R 0RL, England · Penguin Ireland, 25 St Stephen's Green, Dublin
2, Ireland (a division of Penguin Books Ltd) · Penguin Group (Australia), 250 Camberwell Road, Camberwell,
Victoria 3124, Australia (a division of Pearson Australia Group Pty Ltd) · Penguin Books India Pvt Ltd, 11
Community Centre, Panchsheel Park, New Delhi—110 017, India · Penguin Group (NZ), Cnr Airborne and
Rosedale Roads, Albany, Auckland 1310, New Zealand (a division of Pearson New Zealand Ltd) · Penguin
Books (South Africa) (Pty) Ltd, 24 Sturdee Avenue, Rosebank, Johannesburg 2196, South Africa · Penguin
Books Ltd, Registered Offices: 80 Strand, London WC2R 0RL, England

Library of Congress Cataloging-in-Publication Data
Hausman, Gerald.
Horses of myth/by Gerald and Loretta Hausman; illustrated by Robert Florczak.—1st ed.
p.   cm.
Contents: The Arabian: Abjer, the horse of the Saharan sands—The mustang: Snail, the horse of the
American plains—The Mongolian pony: Humpy, the horse of the Russian steppes—The timor: Ghost
Chaser, the horse of the Tahitian shadows—The karabair: Kourkig Jelaly, the horse of the Armenian
Highlands.
ISBN 0-525-46964-8
1. Horses—Folklore. 2. Tales. [1. Horses—Folklore. 2. Folklore.]   I. Hausman, Loretta.
II. Florczak, Robert, ill.   III. Title.
PZ8.1.H29 Ho 2005
398.24'5296655—dc21   2002040809

Published in the United States by Dutton Children's Books,
a division of Penguin Young Readers Group
345 Hudson Street, New York, New York 10014
www.penguin.com/youngreaders

Designed by Richard Amari

Manufactured in China · First Edition
1 3 5 7 9 10 8 6 4 2

For Shai, Taj, and Anais
G.H. & L.H.

For my brothers—Ronald, Michael, and Richard
R.F.

CONTENTS

Introduction

Certain animals, such as cats, dogs, and horses, have been our constant companions since our earliest times on this earth. Each has contributed to our growth as human beings in different ways. The dog has been a faithful guard, friend, and coworker. The cat, besides warming laps and hearts, has kept our food stores safe from rodents. But without the horse's strong back, we couldn't have built the world we know today. For, in the millennia before the motorcar, there was only one way to travel great distances and to haul heavy loads—by horseback.

Mythology explains our relationship with the horse in many ways. It says that we were long ago of horses born, and that as humans we still remember being joined to horses that could fly across the heavens. Mythology also tells us that of the horses of war, none was greater than the dancing Arabian, and of the horses of harmony, none more wing-footed than the Lipizzan. Other horses of greatness were the Percheron, mightiest of the strong, and the Thoroughbred, fleetest of the fast.

In the United States, there are a great many myths celebrating the mule. The Poitou mule was said to be "the mule that made America possible." Without this mule's strength and good sense, the mines and mills would not have worked so smoothly. In field and hollow, farm and town, America profited by having the mule. If the horse made us proud, the mule made us prosperous. And how that little cousin of the horse could make us laugh!

Even in today's world the horse is with us still, so much that we often speak of "horsing around," or using "horse sense," or at least "kicking up our heels."

Since the horse is a vital part of human history, language, literature, and sport, one might wonder where and how it all began. *Horses of Myth* seeks to show how the oldest breed on earth, the Arabian, made its name on the sands of the Sahara. Its ancestry is as old as the word *Arab*. This was the first warhorse, and the empires of the Hittites and the Babylonians rose and fell to the ominous thunder of Arabian hooves. It was written in the stars and told by the tongues of poets that this horse would "fly without wings and conquer without swords." Truly, feudal wars were sometimes put aside in preference for the breeding of beautiful mares.

For the hardy mustang, the horse of the American plains, we tell the story of the race that stopped a war, a race that ended all others. Few today know that the only native-bred equine in America is the Nez Percé Appaloosa. The curious and mystical tale of Snail features a turn-of-the-century mustang who has something of the Appy in him. But he also comes of ancient stock, going back to the Arabian and the Spanish Barb.

The tale of Humpy, the magic horse of Russia, is told around the world. This is the horse of changes, the shape-shifting equine who teaches humanity how to be hopeful—for though humans may stumble and fall, horses trudge on through time, unaware of losses or gains. Little Humpy is the horse of all seasons, coming from a long line of rugged-boned ancestors bred by Genghis Khan. This is the Mongolian Pony whose ability to withstand any climate won her the reputation of being the hardiest of all horses. Moreover, it was her milk and her love of running that gave men in the Gobi Desert sustenance of body and soul.

Ghost Chaser, the Timor found on the island of Tahiti, is another horse of myth. The Timor probably goes back to the legendary Captain Cook, who brought Cape Horses to the Tahitian islands from the Dutch settlements of New Holland. According to the painter Paul Gauguin, the horses of Tahiti lent a certainty to the lonely roads and trackless paths of the wave-washed coastline. Then, too, as our story shows, the tough Timor was unafraid of ghosts—*tupapaus*—who ranged the woodland shadows and made haunts of every human habitation. More than once, the Timor saved Gauguin from losing his way at night in the shadows of the ghostly mountain.

Most mythical of all is the Karabair, the great warhorse of David of Sassoun. The tale of David is as old as the myth of Gilgamesh—as old, perhaps, as the spoken word itself. It was not written down until the nineteenth century, and portions of it still exist in the highlands of Armenia as ballads that travel on the tongue. Here was the mythic, heroic horse that shaped the leader of Armenia and made a strong nation grow into a stronger one. In this tale, we see why the horse has had such a huge influence on humankind. For not only does the equine carry us on its back, but it has also carried us in the flow of its thoughts.

Mythologically, horses have always had the gift of speech and the ability to reason with us. According to our oldest stories, horses could speak before we could. Why? Because in the beginning, we were half human, half horse.

And some of those old equine urgings are still there, daring us to reach for the stars—and sometimes telling us to *become* stars. For as we go into space, we also look back and remember that age-old rocket of ribs and hooves—Pegasus, who lights our way to the heavens. Who reminds us of the entire horse family—racers, jumpers, carriers, herders, healers, and stealers of the human heart.

HORSES
of
MYTH

THE
Arabian

ABJER,
the Horse of the Saharan Sands

Long before you were born, in the days when water was more cherished than gold and horses were more valuable than fire, there lived a boy named Antar. His dream of horses carried him far and wide, though in truth he never left the black, goat-haired tent of his harsh master, Prince Shas of Arabia.

Antar was the prince's personal horseboy, and as such, he was treated as the lowliest of the lowly. The sands under his master's sandaled feet were more highly regarded than Antar, but all the same, the boy bore his suffering silently and with such humility that Shas never knew Antar thought him to be a cruel tyrant.

However, at night, with his duties done and his master asleep, Antar lay under the fiery heavens, fully awake. "Only the stars of the desert are more numerous than the thoughts in my head," Antar whispered to himself. "Oh, how filled with longing am I, and how deeply I wish to ride on a mare's back and to feel the desert storm unfurl about my spurred heels. I was born to be a warrior, not a slave. And it was only chance that I was stolen from my father's people when I was a babe in arms."

Then, telling himself that one day it would all be different, Antar drifted off to sleep. He dreamed of horses . . . of manes flying in the wind like flags, of horses that drank the wind like water . . . of bright hooves that were round and flat as beaten coins . . . of stallion's eyes that were deeper than the deepest well.

In his dreams he was a rider of the finest blooded horseflesh. However, when Antar awoke, there he was—just a barefoot boy who belonged to an arrogant prince, and whose first task of the morning was bathing his master's feet.

One night, though, Antar dreamed that the feet he washed were his own. His master was yelling at him, "Bathe my feet, you insolent boy!" But Antar, in the dream, wiggled his toes in the warm water of the engraved bronze water bowl and smiled. The prince shook with rage as Antar held up his dripping feet— to be toweled dry by the prince!

Antar awoke at dawn, chuckling over the dream.

That same morning, while the prince lay slumbering in his silken sheets, Antar put on Shas's armor. Then he mounted the prince's swiftest mare and galloped into the desert, alone.

Presently, he came upon a camp with many fine horses and strong, long-legged camels. No one in the camp stirred, so Antar rode in bravely, and with more cleverness than luck, he made off with the fittest of the fittest. He wisely knew that the twenty mares he stole would make no sound, for they were so trained. He rounded them up like a master herdsman and drove them off in a soft puff of desert dust.

All this he did before the stallion could sound his alarm. Deftly, Antar caught him by the halter and led him away, too. The drumming of the horses' hooves sounded like a distant storm to the men of the sleeping camp.

A little later, as Antar neared his own camp, a horseman rushed out of a ravine in the rocks and faced him with drawn sword.

The stranger was cloaked in black robes and sat upon a horse of iron gray. This was the most glorious equine Antar had ever seen. He had an arched neck, fine delicate nostrils, intelligent eyes, and smooth limbs that seemed to have been sculpted. His ears were sharp, his hooves were round, and his tail was set in the air.

The moment Antar saw this magnificent steed, his soul longed to possess him.

His desire was so great, his sense took flight—so much so that he approached the horseman with no object but to commandeer his glorious mount. Little did he know that his life was in danger.

When the dark warrior saw that Antar wasn't at all afraid

of him, he spurred his horse to dance imperiously in a circle around the boy. Around and around the rider raced, proving his skill as a horseman and also proving the mettle of his mount.

Then the warrior cried out, "By the heartbeat of the heavenly stallion, you see now how well met you are!"

"I see that you ride a great horse," Antar replied.

The stranger howled. "Great, you say? This is Abjer, the finest horse on earth! No steed can outrun him."

Antar rose to the challenge—for he knew he had to. A warrior could be bested by words as well as deeds. "By the ring of the spur," he sang back, "you may be right about your mount. But here am I, and what will you do when my men appear over that hill?"

"By the whisk of the donkey's tail, you may be a gilded prince and you may have men of iron behind you, but you cheated when you stole my stallion and mares, for I was bathing at the time."

"By the ring of the double bit, that was your bad luck and my good fortune."

"By the milk of the mare," said the other in a rage, "do you know who I am?" Then he tore off his burnoose headdress and revealed a plum-colored face with a livid white scar.

"By the son of the sire," Antar announced, "you are most unlovely to look at in the morning sun."

"By the meekness of the mare and the stalwartness of the stallion, you are bold and foolish, and soon to die."

"By the carelessness of the colt," said Antar, "it is you who are foolish. For as I said, my men over that wrinkled hill await my command. Soon they will swarm you like ants, and then what will you say?"

"By the gall of the gelding, I will tell them that I am none other than Harith, the greatest knight who ever lived!"

Now it happened then, just as Antar let loose his battle cry, that a skirl of wind-driven sand rose up and descended over them.

"By the charger's challenge," shouted Harith in surprise, "you weren't lying—there is a band of men over there!"

And so, in anger and disgust, he surrendered his stock. Yet that was not enough for Antar, who now demanded Harith's unequaled mount. As was the custom when overtaken, Harith gave up his treasured horse, but not without a vow of vengeance.

"By the noise of the nostril," he swore, "you shall pay dearly for this outrage."

And that was how Antar became a man of greatness. With a fortune in royal plunder—horses and camels—and with his horse Abjer, he became the man of the moment. All sang praises to him, and he sang praises to himself, as was the custom. His freedom was neither purchased nor courted, but given freely as was the custom when bravery and warriorship were praised before the council fires at night.

His own poem celebrating his conquest went like this:

> *My life is blessed by fortune,*
> *My fate etched in stars.*
> *I care nothing for danger*

Nor Harith's petty scars.
I ride my horse named Abjer,
The fastest of his breed;
Horse of dreams, I call him,
My night-faced, glowing steed.

In the end it was Prince Shas whose voice was heard above all the rest. He commanded silence and respect. "Wise is the one between whom and Antar there is no contention," he told everyone, knowing that Antar would bring great honor to his name.

The years passed and Antar grew both great and strong, just as Shas said he would. His terrible cry struck fear into the cowardly and the courageous. Of his peerless horse, Abjer, legends spread far and wide. In the campfires of the thousand and one nights there were stories of a horse finer than gold and a rider of moon-pale nights whose deeds were known by all.

One storyteller said it like this: "Abjer is an eagle, a lion with hooves. He darts like a flash of lightning, a tearing arrow. His eyeballs glow red as molten stars and his teeth shine like moonfire. He shrieks and strikes terror into all his foes, so that an approaching army, hearing him cry, will be thrown to the sand by their mounts. Then Antar rushes in and slays them, each and every one."

So it would go until another rival teller of tales tried his tongue at the art of exaggeration: "The true question is whether Abjer is possessed of Antar, or the other way around. Which, then, I ask, is the prince of men, and which the prince of

horses? Are they not equally dangerous in the sight of our enemies? And therefore, they are one, not two. No emperor can
boast of such allegiance, such union. Five hundred angry horse-
men are but a grain of sand before the wind of Abjer, the rain
of Antar."

In the passage of time, Antar fell in love with a woman
named Abla. The daughter of a desert trader, she was as pretty
as Antar was brave. The sweet trouble of love was in both of
them, and they fell deeply into it.

One day when Antar had laid countless treasures at her father's doorway, Abla said in a teasing voice, "Where is my share
of this goodness . . . is it all for my father? Am I of no conse-
quence in the matter?"

"By the light of your heavenly eyes," Antar said, "I give all
this gladly to your father. Yet to you, I give my heart."

Abla loved hearing his praises, and she asked for more. "Is
that all you have to say?" she asked sweetly. "Can you not be
more poetical? Listen, now, to me."

And Abla, who was a skilled poetess, gave Antar something
to think about. "When I view your coming," she said with a
smile, "I see—not horse and man, but rather a mountain range,
sun-bright and carpeted with snow. Gifts? I have no need of
them, for I treasure words over fineries. What words have you,
my dear Antar? Have you no emerald phrases for the one you
say that you adore? Or is your adoration mere courtesy?"

Antar, somewhat taken aback, hastened to say, "You have no
need of words, for you yourself are the holy book of heaven."

"Can you not say more?" she teased. As was the custom, her

asking was his command. If she demanded poetry, then it was verses of the heart he must deliver ... yet he could think of none.

"No," he replied. "I shall presently say something else. ..." His mind sought the phrase, and it came to him. "Perfumes you do not need," he said breathlessly, "for the perfume of your presence overpowers all earthly fragrances."

"Very well," she said at last. "You are better with swords than words. But you have done yourself justice. Do you not want to hear why I love you, Antar?"

He hastened to say that, indeed, he did.

She wrapped a dark curl around her little finger and let it go.

"I love you for the deep well of your heart in the dry year of the desert's drought. ... I love you for the warmth of your smile when the winter wind tears at the wool of the sheep. ... I love you ..." Here she paused, wondering, searching. "Because," she added, "you are still that brave boy who once stole a horse instead of bathing his master's feet."

Thus did Antar woo the lovely Abla; and thus did they both win each other with poetry; and thus were they married. The years went by, and children came to Antar and Abla. Still, Antar's fame as a warrior continued to spread beyond the sands of Syria, beyond the palms of Byzantium, and farther than the courtyards of the Alhambra.

It was said that he and his horse could ride over the moon as easily as a gazelle steps over a stone. It was said that white lions attended his sleep, watching over him, and that jackals grew sweet-tempered under his gaze. Abjer, went the tale, had the face of a man, the mind of a monarch, and spoke with a human voice when he wished to confide with Antar. He had no need of hooves, legend said. He flew, wingless, as when dream carries the body swiftly through the night and one wakes in a different land.

Finally, Antar and Abjer were so well known that their story was inscribed in a mosque in the sacred city of Mecca. But the hour is written, too, when all men must meet their Maker, and death comes to heroes and saints as well as vagabonds and thieves. The way it happened to Antar was like this:

There was one warrior whose fame came near to rivaling Antar's; his name, of course, was Harith. One night when Antar was camped along the Euphrates, Harith hid in the reeds and waited for a glimpse of his old enemy. When morning came and the sky burned red, Harith craned his neck and saw a horse blacker than ebony and more magnificent than myrrh. Harith said, "This is Abjer, my horse! The thief, Antar, took him from me long ago, and made himself famous by doing so. Long have I suffered ignominy at the hand of this man who was, they say, a slave who polished boots. Well, now may he polish boots in heaven."

Harith waited for the time when Antar emerged from his tent to greet the day with prayer—and at that moment, he let fly a well-aimed arrow, for which Antar was utterly unprepared. The arrow, laden with poison, struck him deep. He staggered and fell against Abjer. "Abjer, my faithful," he whispered weakly, "let me hold on to your mane while you bring me back into my tent to die."

Mortally wounded, Antar told Abla his last wish. "I see by the notched feathers that this killing arrow is that of my old enemy, Harith. The man from whom so long ago I gained my great horse, Abjer. Now, at last, he has evened the score, and though I die, I shall live a little longer in your honor, Abla."

"What do you mean, my love?" asked Abla as she cooled his hot brow with a damp cloth.

"Dress in my armor and ride out of camp on Abjer," said Antar. "The sight of my sword in the sunlight and the proud dance of Abjer's hooves will draw Harith to you like a bee to honey."

Abla nodded. "I understand, dearest," she answered. "But then when I have drawn him here, what shall I do?"

Feeling his spirit fading fast, Antar whispered his plan to Abla, and then he died quietly. At the moment of his death, Abjer neighed so loudly that Harith stopped in his tracks alongside the Euphrates where he was camped.

"My enemy is dead," he said to his bodyguard, Nejim.

"How do you know?"

"Do you not feel it? Let us ride now and take back my horse. The time has finally come for my revenge."

And so he gathered one hundred of his best fighting men. They went forthwith to Antar's camp. But before they got there, a rider came between them and the sun.

Nejim said to his master, "I see Antar in full armor mounted upon his warhorse, Abjer. I thought you said you killed him."

Harith spat forth some oaths of rage. Then he collected himself and said, "Fool, can't you see it is a woman underneath that weight of armor? I did kill him, and this is another of his tricks. However, it is his last."

Saying that, he signaled his men to advance. But Nejim told him, "Sire, if you are wrong and it is Antar, we hundred shall suffer defeat at his hands alone."

"I tell you, it is a trick!" swore the furious Harith.

"Do you really believe Antar's wife could wear such unbearable armor? It must weigh over two hundred stone."

"I say whatever my eyes say," vowed Harith, and he kept on riding. His men followed, though with less speed.

When they were quite near to the lone horseman, Harith cried, "Look, men! It is neither Antar's lofty figure nor his manly bearing. What I see—and I doubt it not—is the body of a woman. Do you see how the weight of the iron burdens her frail limbs? Truly, I say, Antar is dead where I laid him low with my arrow."

"We are not so sure, Harith," said the lead tribesman of his council. "It looks like Antar to us." The other mounted men, with their lances across their saddles, agreed.

Now the sand glowed like fire. Inside her prison of armor, Abla was burning up. Stinging sweat blinded her. Finally she couldn't stand it anymore; she removed her iron visor.

In a heartbeat, Harith and his warriors saw the shining face of a beautiful woman.

Nejim said loudly, "The master is right. That is the wife of the slain."

"Attack at once," rasped Harith.

There was a great neighing of horses and a flashing of swords. Then there was a thundering of the many mounted tribesmen. They swept down on Abla like a dark storm.

For the rest of that day, they chased Abla. The sun pounded. The hooves drummed. But none drew near the distant rider. Abjer kept the pace of a demon, and he broke the ranks of the pursuers, one by one, as their mounts collapsed dead in the sand.

At last, there were only the two pursuers—Harith and Nejim.

Abla rode at sundown into the Valley of the Gazelles. And there, for the first time in his life, Abjer stumbled and fell. And lay perfectly still.

The wondrous horse was dead.

Or so it seemed.

Abla, lying on the sand, trying to coax Abjer to his feet, cried as the two men advanced. They descended like vultures, their capes spread into wings.

Then Abla stood with her husband's sword, facing her enemies. "Whatever happens," she said to herself, "Antar is at my side." She raised her sword, and it clanged against the weapon of Harith. Behind came Nejim.

"Say your final prayers," cried Harith as he made his charge.

Yet, as he swung his sword in the setting sun and was about to cut Abla in half, a cry came from behind him. He swiveled in his saddle to see Abjer risen from the sand. Underneath his hooves, in a puddle of wine-colored blood, was Nejim.

"Must I fight you, too, my beauty?" said the astonished Harith. And he whirled to face Abjer.

However, Harith's tired horse was not nimble enough to get out of the way. Abjer's hooves rang on metal and rended flesh. Harith and his horse went down in a heap of iron and bones.

When it was over, Abjer sang the victory song.

Abla thanked the great horse for saving her life, then she removed Abjer's saddle and set him free.

Now they say that Abjer still lives in the Valley of the Gazelles. You can hear his hoofbeats, if you listen. He wears no saddle except that made by the white of the moon on the nights when Antar and Abla walk at his side with their hands entwined. They say this happens once in five hundred years . . . which is but one hour in the land of shadows.

AFTERWORD

This tale goes back to the Arabic folklore of *The Thousand and One Nights,* which was told for centuries by Islamic people before it was written down sometime in the fourteenth century.

Antar is a romantic hero, an epiclike figure, and his horse Abjer is the perfect Arabian warhorse. The intelligence ascribed to Abjer follows the doctrine of the prophet Mohammed, who said that above all animals, horses were sacred. He said the horse would spread the faith to the four corners of the world.

According to Islamic belief, Mohammed was the one who said that the horse was created by Allah before He formed Adam and Eve. It was God's will that man's needs should be provided for even before his coming.

Spiritually, the Arabian horse was made of blessings from on high. Physically, this great equine exhibited them. The Arabian horse was condensed from the South Wind and colored dark bay or chestnut. The *jibbah,* or "bulging forehead," contained the goodwill of God, and so did the *mitbah,* the arching neck with high crest that was the sign of courage. The high tail was the flag of pride.

All in all, the perfectly composed Arabian was God's gift, and it was prized more highly than an Arab's own children. Therefore the intention of all Middle Eastern horse breeders was to keep the breed *asil,* or pure. They did this for hundreds of years.

The tale of Antar and Abjer shows how the well-mounted Bedouin carried out surprise attacks, stealing horses and camels and making his clever escape. Although mares were excellent mounts for raiding parties, as they didn't nicker and warn the enemy of an approach, stallions like Abjer were fierce foes on the battlefield. In the Bible (Job 39: 21–22), the Arabian horse ". . . goeth on to meet the armed men. He mocketh at fear, and is not affrighted; neither turneth he back from sword."

THE
Mustang

SNAIL,
the Horse of the American Plains

One hundred years ago there was a horse named Snail, a sleepy, sulky, and generally lazy mustang. Not that there was anything wrong with that, really, but in the little corner of big Montana where Snail lived, horses were prized for their looks and their speed.

All that was lost on poor Snail.

Oh, he had the noble Barb and the blooded Arabian in his ancestry, but so well hidden. Somehow, the sloping rump and convex head, the pretty, wide-set eyes, small muzzle, and pointed ears were buried in hard-caked dirt, which was just one of the reasons he got the name Snail.

You see, he liked to roll when it rained; and he liked to dust himself when it didn't. It didn't matter how often he was curried, for he had a longing for the creek bottom and its sticky, slicky Montana mud.

Snail was mostly mustang as far as pedigree goes, but at a distance, all muddy and spattered and gone to seed, he seemed nothing more than a leaf-brown horse with a few Appaloosa spots on his hindquarters.

There was nothing that stood out about Snail except that he lived up to his name—he didn't move a muscle except to munch prairie grass or take a roll in the creek bottom.

Well, he did have one peculiarity. Snail's owner, Uncle Bill Wooten, a pioneer in the area, discovered it one day when he was returning from his garden with some fresh-picked vegetables under his arm. He'd just passed Snail when the darn-fool horse took off after him.

Snail was thirty yards off when Uncle Bill noticed that he was about to get run over. Not knowing what else to do, Uncle Bill threw the cabbage head he was carrying and headed straight for his cabin alongside Sourdough Creek. When he looked back a moment later, Snail was happily crunching down the cabbage.

"Well, well," said Uncle Bill, amused. "Snail found something in this topsy-turvy world worth running for—and, if I do say so myself, what a run!"

The next thing Bill did was call some of his friends. He asked Doc Allen, Jeremiah Johnson (the famous mountain man), and Tom McGirl to have a look at his silly, little mustang, the

one everyone thought was a useless pony. They came over the very next day.

Snail, for his part, paid no attention to the men gathered around him. Ignoring everyone, he went on with his munching and crunching.

"Well, what's so special about this not-so-special horse of yours?" queried Doc Allen. The others nodded. They had seen all they wanted to see of Snail.

Uncle Bill explained, "Remember how you fellows wanted to find a racehorse that could beat Plenty Coups' famous buckskin mare?"

Jeremiah Johnson guffawed so loudly a raven coughed in a nearby tree. "You're not gonna tell me that this here hoss of yours can run, are you, Bill?"

Uncle Bill looked slyly at his friends.

Jeremiah picked up a little clod of earth. Uncle Bill undid Snail's tether and held his halter for a moment while Jeremiah sent the clod of dirt flying like a bee. It nipped Snail in the flank, and old Snail—or young Snail—shivered and wiggled his hind end ever so slightly, and went back to grazing buffalo grass. The incident had passed without his knowing it.

"All right," said Tom McGirl, pushing back his Stetson. "What kind of a trick you think you're pulling, Uncle Bill?"

"Yeah," said Jeremiah. "What'd you get us over here for?"

"Time to 'fess up, Wooten," added Doc Allen.

Uncle Bill grinned like a fox. Then he dipped his hand into his feed bag and produced a big, round, green head of cabbage.

"Okey-dokey, Doc, you hold Snail's halter, but you better

let go kind of quicklike when I git to that big fallen tree over yonder."

Off went Uncle Bill, striding like a fireman on the way to a burning schoolhouse. When he got to the fallen log, he called out, "Here, Snail, come to Uncle Bill!"

Then he brandished the cabbage.

At once, Snail kicked up his heels. Then his hooves pummeled the earth, and he took off like lightning. He made it across the pasture before Uncle Bill could lower his hand. In fact, Snail stole the cabbage right out of the air—because Uncle Bill tossed it for fear of being trampled to death.

When Snail was finished chomping and the men were finished staring in amazement, Uncle Bill asked them, "Think we can get ten to one?"

"I think we might git a hunnerd to one," Jeremiah stated.

"Them's odds I like," said Tom with a smile.

"Are you thinking what I'm thinking?" asked Uncle Bill.

Doc Allen rubbed his chin thoughtfully. "I'd say it's time I mosey over to the Crow Indian camp and have a little talk with Plenty Coups. He thinks his buckskin can beat anything on four legs, and there's no reason to disabuse him of that notion."

"We've had . . . how many races against that buckskin?" Jeremiah asked.

"I'd say, ten for a guess," Doc answered, "and we lost all of 'em."

"That buckskin's got spunk and fire for blood," said Tom.

"But Snail'll take her in a stretch . . . long as I have a cabbage head in my hand," Uncle Bill added.

So Doc Allen drove his buggy over to Plenty Coups' camp, and he asked his old friend straightaway if he wanted to run his mare in another race. It never occurred to Doc he'd say no.

But he did.

"To win is good," said Plenty Coups. "To *always* win is bad."

"Well, the way I figure it," said Doc, "to always think you're gonna win is bad. To *sometimes* think you're gonna lose is good."

"What makes you believe there's a horse in the territory that can challenge my buckskin?"

"Doesn't matter what the horseflesh is, as long as we have our annual get-together. You know, every year when the leaves turn gold, we have a horse race. It's sorta traditional."

Plenty Coups grinned. He knew tradition.

"All right," he said, "one more race. But after this . . ."

He didn't finish. He just looked off toward the Pryor Mountains and smiled, as if he were planning a trip there soon.

"You mean," asked Doc in surprise, "that this'll be the last horse race?"

And Plenty Coups nodded.

Well, the day of the race came around as quick as the first Montana frost. In other words, it was right there before you knew it. Sourdough Creek was jam-packed with people—settlers and cowboys on one side of the road, and the whole Crow Nation on the other.

Plenty Coups came in on a white horse, but his son Ironeyes rode the great and gorgeous tan mare that everybody called Buckskin. Her color was soft as sand and brown as dirt. Plenty Coups let everyone admire her, too—her shining muscled coat, her sidestepping, softly neighing, prancing-hoofed beauty. All the Indians sighed when they saw her dance up a little dust. Then they laughed when they saw what the settlers and cowboys and miners and trappers were going to run against her—pathetic, little Snail!

Poor, pitiful Snail had rolled in some mud that morning, and Uncle Bill had left the splotches sticking to his hair. Indecorous little nag that he was, Snail never looked up. He just kept filling his craw while the Crows circulated around him, chuckling and laughing and making fun.

Plenty Coups shook his head. "This is worse," he said to Ironeyes, "than last time."

Ironeyes smoothed the eagle feathers that were braided into the buckskin's mane, and he stroked her lovely white-streaked nose. "I wonder why they like to lose so much," he said.

"Because it makes them happy to see us win," Plenty Coups answered. "Anyway, we shall never know what strange things lie in the hearts of these people. They are as much a mystery to us as we are to them."

No one urged the Crows to place their bets. They did so willingly, even wildly. They dropped down treasure after treasure on the big blanket where the bets were laid. There were pelts and plews and beaded belts and moccasins of all shapes and sizes.

To the Crows the race was already won; a mere formality awaited the dividing of the gifts. Their eyes were fixed on the goods laid out by Uncle Bill and the others: bags of flour, coffee beans, rock candy, ax heads, mirrors, beads, nails, cottons and flannels.

Then the oldest wife of Plenty Coups came forward. She carried a huge white grizzly-bear skin, which she let drop upon the betting blanket like an armful of snow. All eyes—both white and Indian—were on that pretty bearskin.

Doc Allen smiled. Not to be outdone, he dropped a brand-new Pendleton blanket and a Remington saddle rifle on top of the white grizzly fur.

Next, the horses were led to the starting rope. Snail trudging, as if to his death. The buckskin prancing, as if she might dance up to the sun. While the two lined up, Uncle Bill Wooten felt inside of his coonskin cap, which was laid across his arm. Then he walked down to the end of the track and waited for the race to begin.

Plenty Coups took his place beside him.

The buckskin was reined up at the starting rope by Ironeyes.

Snail was walked up by the son of the owner of the Sourdough Trading Post, a light-boned youth everybody called Wee Willy. Now, Willy *was* small. But he was also the best rider in the territory.

Anyway, there they were, ready to ride the race of their lives—if, of course, the horses were willing. Well, one of them was . . . at least that was the way it looked.

Plenty Coups peered into Uncle Bill's coonskin cap.

"What do you call that?" he asked.

"Medicine," replied Uncle Bill. "What do you call *that?*"

Plenty Coups held up a string with some pale fur on it.

"This is the white tip of the silver foxtail."

Uncle Bill asked, "You think that thing'll win the race?"

Plenty Coups chuckled. "It won't hurt. Do you think your vegetable can defeat my foxtail?"

"It won't hurt," Uncle Bill replied.

Then the two of them smiled at each other, right up until the moment the rope was dropped and the gun was fired, and the race began.

Uncle Bill held up his cabbage so Snail could see it.

Plenty Coups waved his foxtail tip.

All eyes were on that little, sleepy-eyed Snail because, although he was behind by a length, he was catching up.

Then they were neck and neck, Wee Willy leaning almost level with Snail's neck.

The buckskin, that magnificent sun-dancing mare, edged up by a head. Ironeyes clung tight, quirting his mount.

Uncle Bill thrust out his head of cabbage.

Plenty Coups swung his foxtail string in a circle, singing softly under his breath. The settlers screamed and the Indians wailed, and the two horses drummed the earth so loudly the golden leaves on the cottonwoods floated off their branches and rained down on everyone's head.

And the horses came on with a rumble that made the earth tremble.

Their feet were striking now in timed precision. The buckskin snorting, Snail blowing froth. Both galloping for all they were worth. And then the mud-spotted, begrimed little Snail inched up, with Wee Willy stuck to his back like a burr.

"By golly, that queery-eyed, little Snail's gointer win!" cried a prospector.

"No chance," said a tall, blanketed Crow, who cheered Iron-eyes on.

They were almost at the finish line when Buckskin came up ahead of Snail once again. On came Snail—the cabbage well in view. And then, well, that little nose length of his might've won the race. . . .

It just might've.

But who could really tell?

You see, the race all happened so fast. And then the strangest thing of all occurred.

A dust devil rose up off the plains. It spun a tower of white. It billowed up and dropped down, and it settled on the crowd and blinded them.

Now, when the dust cloud cleared, the people were fighting over who was the winner—the buckskin or Snail. The people were divided on two sides of the road. They were shaking fists at one another, and it looked as if a real battle was going to break out on Sourdough Creek.

Amid the dust and confusion, barking dogs, crying children, nickering horses, angry oaths, and victory whoops, the people fell back into their separate camps to decide what to do.

"Did you see the winner?" Doc Allen asked Uncle Bill.

Uncle Bill said, "I saw it as a tie."

"They were neck and neck—till that dust devil smoked us out," said Tom McGirl.

Doc Allen added, "Snail had the buckskin by a nose, as I see it, or saw it, or the way it *seemed* to have happened. How about you, Jeremiah, what'd you see?"

Jeremiah looked a long way off into the smoky plains, and beyond them, to the far blue mountains. Then he surveyed the two warring camps of angry men and women alongside Sourdough Creek. If something wasn't decided soon, he just knew the racetrack was going to turn into a battlefield.

He ran his hands through his whitish-brown, shoulder-length hair and shook it out. It amused him to see that everyone was equally covered with alkali dust. Even little Snail and the broad-chested buckskin had gone from gray to white and from brown to white. But as to the race's outcome, Jeremiah was as stumped as the rest, and he said, "Hell's bells if I know."

Plenty Coups showed up then, his face white as snow. "Who do you make the winner to be?" he asked Uncle Bill, who screwed up his face and smacked his lips and replied, "One or t'other, I suppose."

Then Plenty Coups grinned. "I thought Snail was a loser. But now I know different. Snail is a Thunder Horse."

Uncle Bill brightened. "So you have him as the winner?"

Plenty Coups answered, "I have him as a Thunder Horse."

Jeremiah, edging in, asked, "So you think Buckskin's the winner?"

"I think it shall soon be decided," Plenty Coups said, his grin all gone.

"I certainly hope so," Doc Allen interjected. "Whoever wins is going to be rich as Caesar."

"Was he a great horse racer?" Plenty Coups asked.

"No," said Tom McGirl, "but he was a pretty fair gambler."

"I see," said Plenty Coups.

Then the five of them stood and looked at the treasure that was heaped up on the blanket, piled three feet high—the furs and hides, the jewelry, the store goods and foodstuffs.

The crowd of cowboys and miners and trappers were all arguing and shaking fists at the Crows, who were making hostile gestures. Any minute, a bloody fight was going to break out.

It was at this moment that Plenty Coups stood between the two groups and raised his hand. It took a little while for things to get quiet, but they finally did. Then the only sound was the snorting of the two racehorses and the cry of the magpies in the golden cottonwood trees.

Plenty Coups began by saying, "Listen with your hearts, all of you." His sharp eyes found every face in the two crowds. The people grew even quieter, so that the breathing of the horses was all that could be heard. Lazily the wind raised some more of the white talcum dust and dropped some more leaves of sun-minted gold. But no one said a word.

Plenty Coups spoke again.

"We are all," he explained, "as the Great Mystery made us, men and women, horses and dogs, birds and leaves, and grass and dust. These fine things spread out on the blanket mean little to us, those of us who have the life given to us by the Great Mystery. That life I speak of is all that there is and all that there will be in this time. So, I say now, take these things, these bits of silver and gold, and keep them. This is my decision, and I have spoken."

"Who . . . who shall take them?" Uncle Bill asked.

Plenty Coups answered, "Let those who have no dust on their face take away the winner's blanket and all that lies upon it."

Now the people hearing this looked from one to the other and all around, and up and down. But, of course, there was no such person unmet by dust. Each and all were dusted up and dusted down. And all were equals under the sun, including the two horses, who still pranced about the creek with their riders trying to rein them in.

"Is there no winner, then?" Uncle Bill asked Plenty Coups, who answered, "We are all winners and losers from the day we are born." The big grin was back on his face as he finished, "We are winners coming in, we are losers going out. In between, we are glad to be alive." He made a motion for his people to pack up and leave, which they did, but no one made a move to collect the glitter on the blanket that lay in the sun.

"Well, sir," said Doc Allen as he saw the cowboys lead off their horses and wagons, and the miners tramp back to the hills, and the trappers follow them on their soft-moccasined feet. After a short while Sourdough Creek looked the way it always had, and the cottonwoods shivered and dropped fine coins on the blanket that lay in the September sun.

It was time to say something, but the four friends who had wound up the race didn't know what. They stood in the desolation of the road and looked at Snail. He looked the same—except a lot whiter—still munching grass and paying no attention to the men.

Uncle Bill still had some cabbage leaves. He let them fall, one by one, and the wind took them to the four corners of the plains. The four friends watched the leaves blow away, but Snail never saw them. And the treasures on the winner's blanket stayed untouched, until the first snows covered them that winter.

And they are there, today, one hundred and ten snows later.

The name of the village that grew up along Sourdough Creek is called Snail's Pace, and it still is a one-horse town.

AFTERWORD

The tale of little Snail happened before the turn of the century. It came out of the Canyon Creek country, near Pryor Pass. Some of the participants were true-to-life heroes who saw the early days of the opening of the West. Perhaps the most famous of these was the man who came to be known as Liver-Eating Johnson, Jeremiah or John Johnston, who died in the Old Soldiers' Home in Los Angeles in 1900. He was one of the West's most legendary mountain men.

Equally famous in his own right was Chief Plenty Coups of the Crow Nation. He was revered by all for his great wisdom and compassion. He solved problems in the same way that King Solomon did in the Bible. That is to say, he allowed for human error, he excused it, but he also let "the punishment fit the crime." After Plenty Coups died, the Crow people refused to choose another chief, as no one could take his place.

Snail came from Oregon and was probably bred from stock that originated with the Nez Percé tribe. Their horses were the only blooded stock that was truly indigenous, which means bred by American Indians. Naturally, all native horses sprang from the mustangs that had been brought to America by the conquistadores. However, various forms of mustang sprang up among the Indians. The best bred of these was the Appaloosa developed by the Nez Percé.

Most likely, since Snail was from that part of Oregon and he had the requisite spots, he was an Appaloosa-and-mustang cross. Such horses were known to have minds of their own. They could be as stubborn as they were hardy and faithful and trail-worthy. Weather didn't bother them; they were excellent runners and herding horses.

The myth of the horse that is sleepy-looking and seems to be unmade for racing is an old one, indeed. Old Bones, the famous racehorse, was just such an example. Awkward and rangy, Old Bones didn't fit anyone's bill for the racetrack. His real name was Exterminator, and he was born in Lexington, Kentucky, in 1915. He won the Kentucky Derby in 1918 as a complete unknown, and then went on to become America's top winner of cup races. Many claim he was the greatest Thoroughbred ever.

Exterminator was real, and so was Snail. Both were unknown before they won their first race. Snail retired early; Bones lasted a good many years. Their common ground was in the way they were changed, mythologized by American legend. Theirs is the story of the archetypal loser who wins big. The horse who didn't care to win in the first place. The horse whose heart was bigger than any of his other features. The horse who loved to smell the flowers. Such horses, and such people, are beloved throughout the world because they seem to be blessed. They have it all before taking a single step.

THE
Mongolian Pony

HUMPY,
the Horse of the Russian Steppes

As it was told in days gone by, there was once a horse master of St. Petersburg whose name was Kasimir. His sons, Daniel and David, were his hope for the future, but his daughter, Sashya, was an insult to his pride . . . and all because she was kind and good and talented.

Was it her fault that she was born a girl?

Or that she resembled her lovely mother, Katya?

And was it not to her credit that, young though she was, she could ride a horse almost as well as he could?

To any reasonable father, these things would have been a just and fruitful blessing. But Kasimir's heart never did beat warmly, and the truth was, he'd always been insanely jealous of his wife, Katya, because of her extraordinary horsemanship. So skillful was she that the Tsar himself admired her and made a favored place for her in his court.

Well, as it happened, Kasimir sought a secret revenge for this affection of the Tsar's. He planned to get rid of Katya, in the hope of having the Tsar's attention all to himself. So, when a sultan in Turkey sold a shipment of trotting horses to the Tsar, Kasimir sent his wife to bring them back to St. Petersburg. She never returned from her journey. The ship was lost, no one knew how or why.

Thereafter, pretending to be deep in mourning, Kasimir forbade mention of his wife's name, and he wouldn't let any of his children ride a horse.

Time passed, and one day Kasimir told his children that a thief had slipped into the royal barn and was stealing the horses' grain each night.

"Which one of my clever children can capture this thief?" he wanted to know.

"What kind of thief?" asked Daniel, who was the eldest.

"The kind that nibbles you out of business."

"Do you mean a mouse?" asked David, who was the youngest.

"I mean," said his father hotly, "a beast much the larger, a creature far more destructive than a mouse."

"Do you mean another horse?" asked Sashya.

"How in the name of the saints could a stabled horse steal from another stabled horse?" asked Kasimir.

"Easily," answered Sashya. "The one who steals does not come from *inside* the stable but rather from *outside*."

All three roared over Sashya's ignorance.

"Nonsense," bellowed the father. "Now go do what you were meant to do—that is, not to think, but to work." And she was ordered to clean the stalls while her older brother, Daniel, went about capturing the thief.

"I think it is a fox," he said to his father, and so he made a fox trap.

But the next morning the trap was empty, and even more grain was gone from the bin. Next, it was David's turn.

"I think it is a badger," he said, and so he set a badger trap.

Yet, when morning came, the trap was unsprung, and still more grain was gone from the bin.

As Sashya was the only one left, Kasimir decided to let her have a try at catching the grain thief. When she finished her chores that evening, she made a hollow in the hayloft and settled deeply into it.

"How can one catch what hasn't been seen?" she reasoned. "First you measure your opponent, then you set your trap."

Though her intentions were good, she soon fell asleep in the warm hay. No sooner had she dozed off than there was a bumping on the barn door.

Sashya snapped awake.

The barn door shuddered—once, twice, thrice.

Then, as if by some incantation, it opened a crack, then swung wide.

Into the straw-scented closeness of the royal stable entered a most unusual guest.

There, all by itself, was a creature half horse and half donkey . . . in size. In appearance, it seemed to be something of a camel, for it had a huge hump on its back.

"Who—I mean, *what* are you?" Sashya asked the little, humpbacked horse, who was already at the grain bin, munching away.

The grain spilled from his teeth, and he said, "I am the ugliest horse you ever saw."

"No horse is ugly," Sashya said.

"How can you say that?" asked the odd little animal.

"Because each and every creature under the sun is as beautiful as the day God made it. But tell me, how is it that you can speak? And what is your name?"

"I am what you see, a misfortune of nature. I am called Humpy by any who should be so unlucky as to see me. My speech is one of my gifts. My other graces you shall soon find out about."

"Such a lovely name," praised Sashya. She studied the strange beast. He had the sturdy legs of a draft horse and the tiny head of a colt. His coat was dapple gray; his mane and tail the color of gunpowder. Well, he *was* queerly made. But his eyes were large and kind, and they looked like amber from the sea.

"Your speech is a wonderful thing!" Sashya replied. "But your eyes even outshine your words."

"You make me feel almost like a real horse," said the little creature gratefully.

"I wonder how can I persuade my father to let me keep you?" Sashya said.

"Oh, I'd be terribly out of place here," Humpy told her. "But

I must tell you this—whosoever can ride me will be endowed with my powers."

"You have *powers?*"

"True. For all my great ugliness, I *am* a magic horse."

"My father won't permit any of us to ride, but I secretly do so, anyway. There is nothing on God's earth that I cannot ride," said Sashya. "I believe this gift came from my mother, who was the best horseman in all of Russia."

"I must warn you—I've never been ridden before," said Humpy. "Still, I have hope that one day, someone will do so."

Sashya accepted the challenge.

After walking around Humpy a couple of times, she wasn't sure quite how to mount him.

"Where do I put my legs?" she asked.

"Don't ask me," Humpy answered, still eating. "And if you do get on, watch out for my hump."

Seeing no other way, Sashya took hold of his ears and wrapped her legs around his neck.

"Shall we start, then?" he asked.

"Anytime you're ready."

Humpy exploded like a tiny volcano. Sashya's fingers slipped through his unruly mane, she bounced off his hump, and she fell to the ground.

"Will you try again?" he asked.

This time, Sashya mounted him backward. She grabbed his tail instead of his mane. She wrapped her legs around his belly, pressed hard with her knees.

But Humpy rattled her loose with one good buck.

Sashya struck the floor with a thud.

"Will you try once more?"

Sashya dusted herself off. Then she climbed on Humpy's back, sitting just behind his hump. Her arms went around it, her hands clasped on the other side.

This time when Humpy bolted, pitched, fishtailed—and even twirled like a top—Sashya stayed on. He bounced and jounced; he pumped and pounced. And, still, Sashya stayed on. He couldn't, for the buck of him, shake her. She stuck like glue.

"Well," said Humpy, sucking wind, "you've proven yourself to be the best rider in Russia. Now I'll have to prove my magic to you."

"Right now, I hope."

"In time, your hope will come true."

Sashya said, "I used to hope for the best, always, and it was often granted . . . that was when my mother was around. But now my father runs things. He doesn't like girls."

"I hope he'll like me."

"*That* may be too much to hope for," Sashya said.

"*Nothing* is too much to hope for—even when you're an ugly little horse. I hope all the time that one day, I'll look altogether different."

"Well, to me, you already do."

"Now, *that* is hopeful thinking!"

The next morning, when Kasimir learned that his daughter had caught the grain thief and wanted to keep him, he was furious.

"We should, by right, send that nag to the butcher. Though

he'll hardly yield much more than soup bones, from the look of him."

"Please, Father, let me keep him. I promise I'll take care of him, just like I take care of all the other horses that belong to the Tsar."

Kasimir answered gruffly, "Your work is to spin flax whenever you have the time, and to make lace. But presently we need seven cords of beech wood and seven months' worth of tallow candles. If you've accomplished these tasks by the morrow, I will let you keep that miserable humpbacked horse."

Daniel and David jeered. Working was bad enough. But doing work in order to keep a pathetic and useless horse was a laughing matter. They split their sides whenever they cast a glance at Humpy.

Sashya ignored her brothers' mean faces and kept to her chores, working steadily through the long, hard day.

By day's end, Daniel asked her, "How can a girl cut seven cords of wood?"

She said, "I really don't know."

And she didn't.

That evening, when she visited Humpy, she said sadly, "I've barely chopped a single cord of beech, and I'm afraid I'm losing hope—we only have till tomorrow morning, you know."

"Climb on my back," Humpy offered. "Let me take you to the most hopeful place that I know."

"I'm too tired to ride anywhere," Sashya answered dispiritedly.

Yet Humpy insisted that to be hopeless was to be defeated before the battle was begun.

So, they went off into the frozen woodland. Overhead, the night was hung with crystal stars, and underfoot, the crisp snow crunched. They sank in, all the way up to Humpy's chin, but still he plowed along, pushing the cold snow with his nose like a mole.

At last they came to a glen where the ice had melted and the air was warm as spring. A soft, secret glow came from the steaming snow. The gentle light brightened the dark trees. Sashya was amazed to see that at the ends of the branches there were buds bursting into leaf.

She had never seen anything like this . . . was it a dream?

"What makes it so warm here?" she whispered.

"Don't you see the feather there?" Humpy asked.

Sashya looked into the melting meadow. It was afire with jewels of dew. They winked gold and green around a red quill of fluffy down as large as an eagle's wing.

"I see a feather of fire," she exclaimed.

Humpy said, "A plume plucked from the tail of the Firebird. As you can see, it turns winter into spring."

"And lights the night like a midnight sun," Sashya said in awe. "May I touch it?"

"Go on, it won't burn you."

She dismounted and got the feather. Wherever she stepped, the snow went away and turned to an apple-scented fog that was warming to the skin and golden to the eye. All about her the white flowers of frost faded and slender green shoots took their place. In a moment the grass was ankle-deep and rich as fur.

"With that feather, you'll surely win over your father," Humpy promised.

"But how can it release me from cutting firewood and making candles?"

"Have you lost hope—so soon?"

"I can't see what good hope, or this funny feather, will do...."

"Trust to hope, dear friend. And why cut wood when you are warmed by a feathery furnace?"

As soon as he said it, Sashya knew that it was true, for wherever the feather went, the woods turned to spring, and thence to summer. The cuckoo sang in their wake, and the song of the thrush answered.

When morning came, Kasimir, Daniel, and David stepped into the barn. They were greeted by a great surprise.

The summery hay was oven-warm. The many-colored horses whinnied in the forgiving air, the dull stalls were draped with sweet-smelling woodbine, and corners were carpeted with the musk of moss.

Best of all, there were colts—baby horses nickering in the winterless wonder of their birth.

All this astonished the three, and they staggered at the beauty of it. But surly Kasimir was quick to recover his composure.

Stroking his chin and eyeing the Firebird's feather, from which sprang the most heat and light, he said, "Now there is a thing of magic, indeed—a feather that is the equal of seven cords of wood and worth much more than two hundred candles of pale tallow."

He shook his head in disbelief.

"Does this mean I can keep my little horse?" Sashya begged to know.

"On that, I will give my answer tonight," Kasimir replied darkly. His intention, though, was to keep the feather and get rid of the daughter and her friend. What did he need them for now that he possessed the magic feather, from which any amount of good might come to him?

When they left the stable, Daniel and David said their worst.

"She's—a witch!" cried Daniel. "Our own sister!"

"That horse is evil," spoke David.

"Is that so?" asked Kasimir.

"Our sister—the witch!" Daniel repeated.

"Devil horse!" sang David.

But a cunning smile crept across their father's lips. "There's no power on earth greater than the sea," he said mysteriously.

"The sea?" asked Daniel, in surprise.

"The large water from which comes our salt fish?" questioned David, dumbly.

"Don't be so doltish!" snapped Kasimir. "I will seize that feather, and then I'll send her and her horse to sea."

Both brothers nodded with only a dim light of understanding in their eyes.

Kasimir left them standing and shaking their heads while he went off, saying to himself, "What worked before shall work again. To sea, to sea, with deviltry!"

That evening after supper, Sashya asked again if she could keep her little horse.

Kasimir coldly eyed the Firebird's feather in the center of

the table. It glittered and sent golden waves of warmth through the small cottage.

"Since you didn't fulfill your task *exactly* as I asked—"

"I did just what you wanted!" Sashya protested. "We have all the heat and light we need!"

"Yes, my child, but where is the beech wood, well cut and neatly stacked? How it would do my heart good to see it so."

Sashya dropped her head. "How can I ever please you, Father?"

"Where are the tallow candles?" he demanded.

She shrugged. "I don't think we need them anymore."

"And who are you to . . . *think?*" hissed Kasimir.

"Leave the thinking to us," chipped in Daniel, who looked wisely at his brother.

"That's right," echoed David, winking.

"Silence," said Kasimir. "Now, Sashya, if you want to keep that horrible little horse, I've one last thing for you to do."

"Tell me," Sashya begged, "and whatever it is, I'll do it gladly."

Kasimir grinned. "Very well, my daughter. I want you to find the finger ring that was once worn by your dead mother. Its stone is milk-white opal. You'll find it off the frozen coast . . . somewhere . . . but who knows where? Now, if you can find the ring and bring it to me, I'll let you keep the humpbacked horse."

Her father's ice-blue eyes twinkled. Well he knew that Sashya, despite whatever magic she seemed to have, couldn't possibly bring back the lost ring. In truth, no one really knew where Katya's ship had sunk . . . not even himself.

Sashya and Humpy journeyed to the coast the very next day, and it was not long before they came to the open sea, which lay so flat, with the beach sand stretching for miles and the weak winter sun dully shining.

Sashya was despondent.

"How are we to find a tiny ring in this great frozen sea?"

"Well," said Humpy, "I can't swim, it's true. But neither of us should ever lose hope. After all, hope is magic."

"Yes, but what are we going to do?"

"I hope . . ." said Humpy, but he never finished. Because, at that moment, they heard a cry.

"Look over there," said Humpy. "Someone needs our help."

On the ruffled, foam-laced sand there was a fat, old sturgeon. He'd been caught by a fisherman, who was now off gathering wood for his cooking fire.

Humpy said, "Quick, save the sturgeon before the fisherman returns."

Sashya did as she was told. Then, when she gently put the sturgeon back into the sea, he turned, and with a flip of his tail, he spoke to them.

"How can I thank you for saving my life?" asked the sturgeon.

"There is one thing," said Humpy. And he told of the lost ring.

"You say it is the color of milk?" the sturgeon questioned.

"The pale color of the moon," mentioned Sashya.

The sturgeon spoke again. "I know a whale who, sometime ago, swallowed a ship."

"Wouldn't that make him sick?" Sashya asked.

"It made him dead," the sturgeon said. Then he went on: "I cannot dive so deep where the bones of the whale lie salt-bleached and still, but I know a dolphin who can go part of the way down, and he knows a burfish who can dive still farther in the dark, and he knows a bream who knows a sheatfish who knows a lobster—"

"Enough of who-knows-who in the sea!" cried Humpy. "Can't you please get to the point?"

"Well, with the help of my brothers and sisters," answered the sturgeon, "I think I can get the box that hides the ring that was in the ship that was swallowed by the whale that is now a skeleton on the bottom of the cold, cold sea."

Forthwith, the grateful sturgeon dived beneath the waves.

Sometime later that day, a little bream fish showed up with something round between his teeth.

"Is it really my mother's ring?" Sashya exclaimed.

"Never give up hope," Humpy said.

"I haven't . . . but . . ."

Indeed, when she held it in her palm, she knew that this was the same moonstone worn by her mother before she died. Sashya cried to see it, and when her hand closed around it, she vowed to make her father keep his promise.

Well, when the two returned home so swiftly, the father and the brothers were most surprised. But nothing could have made them hold their breath as they did when Sashya presented the ring to Kasimir.

He said nothing. He stared.

And, for once, the brothers held their thick tongues.

However, as soon as Sashya and Humpy had gone off to the barn to sleep, Daniel said, "You see, Father, their powers have grown. Now those two are more dangerous than ever."

"Yes," David chimed in, "we'll soon be working for them, I'm sure."

"Silence," said the father. "I have a plan in which they're certain to founder."

"May we know of it?" Daniel pleaded.

"Yes," David squeaked, "may we?"

"Come close," said their father, his eyes glittering, and then he whispered what he had in mind.

Now, in the morning, the brothers prepared a tub of hot milk just as their father had ordered. And Sashya and Humpy were called up to see it.

"We're all set to go to the Tsar and tell him of your powers. But first we have to get the little beast clean. Tell him to step into this copper tub and take a good and proper bath."

Sashya put her finger in the bubbling tub and discovered that it was boiling hot.

"Father, dear Humpy will die in this awful bath!"

"There, there," comforted Humpy. "It's a bath like any other. I'll be all right."

"You don't understand," Sashya whispered with tears in her eyes. "They intend to kill you."

"Nonsense," insisted Humpy. "I've been in hotter stuff than this."

And before Sashya could stop him, the little horse jumped into the scalding bubbles and disappeared into the foam.

At the same time, a handsome man sprang out of the molten milk. And he was singing a song that went:

"This hot won't do, I need cold, too!"

And he dived into the snow and rolled all around. He was laughing and gleaming, and he was dressed like a prince.

When at last he stood up and brushed the snow dust from his finely embroidered white coat, he shook his black hair and cast his amber eyes on all who saw him there.

"At last!" He sighed. "The spell is over."

"Who are you?" cried Sashya. "Where is my little horse?"

"Gone," said the grinning fellow. "Gone like the horrible hump that he had to bear. You see, I am the true son of the Tsar—a prince cast out long ago by a sorcerer whose ambition was to run the palace himself."

"I'll see my hopeful little horse no more?" wept Sashya.

"You'll see him every time you look into my eyes, dear girl. You'll see him whenever you remember his message to you."

Sashya stopped crying and looked up.

"Didn't he say that hope was magic?" asked the prince.

"I hope so," said Sashya, smiling for the first time.

So that was how Sashya, the horse master's daughter, married a prince and became the princess with the moonstone ring. As for her family—Daniel and David made fine stable boys and Kasimir became the best bather of horses who ever held a scrub brush.

As for Sashya, she never looked into her husband's amber eyes without remembering the magic horse of Russia who taught her to hope and to hold magic close to her heart.

AFTERWORD

The story of Humpy, the magic horse of Russia, is common to many cultures. It is similar to "The Frog Prince," "The Fisherman and His Wife," "The Poor Miller's Boy and the Little Cat" by the Brothers Grimm, not to mention "Cinderella" and "Rumpelstiltskin."

As in many Grimm stories, the magic shape-shifting or transformational animal usually has wicked brothers or sisters and a selfish father or stepmother to act as an opposing force of evil. In addition, there is the disadvantaged child, who has been bilked of his or her birthright. Usually, the hero or heroine is given an impossible task that can only be accomplished with the help of the kindly sorcerer, the magical animal, the friend from beyond the grave. All of these elements are suggested in "The Magic Horse of Russia."

The character of Humpy is found in Ireland, too. He is in "The Tangle-Coated Horse," part of the sagas of Finn MacCoul. One might also remember the galloping kelpies of similar fame; these were Celtic horses that were part human and part ghost.

During the eighteenth-century era of Peter the Great, Russia's literature was greatly influenced by tales from other countries, and it is probable that little Humpy came from that time. As a real horse, Humpy seems most like the Mongolian Pony.

This is a rough, sturdy, and primitive wild horse. Historically, these equines were wise warriors on the march. So it's fitting that Humpy shows the character of the Mongolian, the horse that won't give up, no matter what the obstacle—one of the most hopeful horses there is.

T H E
Timor

GHOST CHASER,
the Horse of the Tahitian Shadows

Once there lived an artist by the name of Paul Gauguin, who was sick and tired of living in France. His dream was to be in a place where he could put away his heavy clothes and his dark thoughts. He wished to live in the warm sun on an island where nobody knew his name, and where he could paint in peace. And so he left France and sailed away to Tahiti, and he settled in the small village of Maitaiea. Little did he know that his life would be changed forever—not by Tahiti, but by a horse!

Gauguin had just settled into a little bamboo hut roofed with pandanus leaves and carpeted with fresh, dry grass. His happiness was so great he could hardly get over it, and much of the time he went around mumbling praises.

I'm so happy here in my little hut, he thought. I hear only the beat of my heart and the gentle whickering of my neighbor's horses. If only my old friend Van Gogh might see me now—for this, truly, is what we were seeking—paradise on earth!

So it was that he passed his solitary days, painting pictures of the things he saw around him—the loose black pigs and the small brown horses of his handsome friend Totefa. The horses were, in fact, offspring of the same stock brought to Tahiti decades earlier by the fabled explorer Captain Cook. Tough ponies they were, too—probably of some ancient stock. They were short in stature but round and pleasing to the eye. Like shadows, they appeared and disappeared in the bush. Horses were good to have around. For it was well known that they kept away ghosts.

When Gauguin first asked Totefa if he might paint him and his horse, Totefa agreed with a shy smile. So Gauguin did a portrait of Totefa and Ghost Chaser.

It was one of those days when the light changed very rapidly and the shadows under the palms shifted, going from green to blue and back again to green. It seemed to Gauguin that his subjects, the young man and the horse, were underwater, and the air itself swam with fishes instead of birds.

Finally, when Gauguin had finished for the day, Totefa came around to see the painting. Was he shocked!

Totefa exclaimed, "I look as I am, but what of poor Ghost Chaser? You colored him green!"

As if he, too, wanted to see what he looked like in that color, Ghost Chaser walked over and thrust his big head against the painter's shoulder, almost knocking over his easel.

"Oh, oh," said Gauguin. "You mustn't do that—I could never capture this light again in a thousand years."

Ghost Chaser snorted and wandered off, looking like the very brown horse he was.

"I have never seen a green horse." Totefa laughed.

"And now you own one." The artist grinned.

Totefa looked for a while at the painting. Then he said, "There is a place on the mountain where everything is that color."

"You mean where everything is green?"

"Where things change color before your eyes . . . blue, green, gold, red."

"And where is this magical place, Totefa? I should like to go there and see it for myself."

"That might not be a good idea."

"Why not?"

Totefa looked upward, where the mountain loomed and threw its enormous shadow on the valley.

"Well, you see, there are many Ghost Chasers up there."

"Horses?"

Totefa laughed.

"Ghosts," he said.

"You must take me, then."

"Why?"

"I want to paint them."

"Oh," Totefa said seriously, "you cannot do that."

Gauguin looked puzzled. "And why not?"

"Ghosts are spirits of the forest who do not wish to be seen. If we invade their territory, we must be very careful not to disturb them."

Gauguin shrugged. "I'm not afraid of ghosts," he said indifferently.

"You should be. They can take your life if you displease them."

Gauguin rolled his eyes. "Where I come from," he commented, "there are no ghosts, but there are people who live as if they had no life; so in the end, it comes to the same thing."

Totefa climbed on the back of Ghost Chaser and started to clop off into the rows of slender, thatch-topped palms. The cinnamon color of his skin was just as it was in the painting, but now his horse was golden brown in the sun.

"When will you take me to the mountain of ghosts?" Gauguin called after Totefa.

The young man, turning halfway, faced him with a smile. "Tomorrow, if you're not afraid, and if you promise not to awaken the hungry ghosts up there."

Laughing, Gauguin answered, "I am the hungriest ghost you will ever meet, Totefa."

The youth rode on through the tunnel of tall trees.

The following day, they departed at dawn. Totefa went first.

Gauguin, riding Ghost Chaser, followed closely behind. They took a vertical path that ran steeply into the mountain's heart. On either side of the trail giant ferns spilled over, glistening with diamonds of dew. The forest thickened into ironwood, pandanus, luscious red-blooming hibiscus. The air was blossomy and sweet and scented with strange, earthy fragrances.

After a time, the path disappeared. Totefa swung his ax to clear the way. It was slow going. Gauguin was in no hurry. He admired the tracery of vines, the boiling waters of the creek that bowled down from the heights and tinkled like fine silver in the interlaced streams at the foot of the mountain.

To Gauguin, a city dweller, it smelled primeval. He thought of Eden's ancient garden, lost in the leaves of time.

On horseback, he dreamed himself back to when no human presence darkened the day, to when light tumbled from afar like the rivers of water that came down from the mountain of ghosts.

Finally Totefa stopped at a small clearing.

When Ghost Chaser stopped walking and Totefa stopped chopping, the silence was loud. No bird sang. No cricket chirped. The woods echoed with emptiness.

Gauguin thought he saw the secret movements of unseen animals in the dense, rain-polished leaves. But there was nothing he could really lay his eye on.

"Are there any wild animals up here?"

"I don't know of any," Totefa said, a half smile playing on his lips.

He was wearing only a pareu, or loincloth, and his skin shone brightly in the moist, humid air.

From the earth, a fine mist crept along the ground. Ghost Chaser stomped, eager to be going on. Startled, the little puffs of vapor leaped, then lay down flat and began creeping again.

Gauguin watched Totefa, who stood in a beam of sunlight. He was there for only a second, then, most mysteriously, Totefa seemed to fade away into the shadows. And—just like that—he was back in the sunshine again. Gauguin thought he looked weird, his body strange—as if it didn't belong to him. He looked unlike himself. Not like a boy but like a rough-and-tumble man.

"What is happening?" Gauguin said aloud.

When Totefa answered him, it sounded like he was speaking from within a cave.

Gauguin could barely hear him.

"Are we there," the artist asked, "in the mountain of ghosts?"

Totefa disappeared into a mantle of fog that covered all but his face. Then, that, too, was masked, covered over by the jungle's velvet soft cloak.

Gauguin felt quite alone.

He gripped Ghost Chaser with his knees.

"What is it I'm seeing?" he asked himself. "What is going on here?"

Then he hollered Totefa's name at the top of his lungs. Immediately the boy stepped out of the low clouds. He was smiling.

"I lost you for a moment there," Gauguin said. He heard his heart pound. His breath came in gasps.

"That happens up here," Totefa told him. "Don't be frightened."

"Me, frightened? I'm never that way!" Gauguin said defensively.

Totefa said nothing, but he began gathering firewood from around the banks of the limpid pool, which, at its upper end, was fed by a waterfall. The steep sides of the mountain rose vertically from behind the pool. The shadow it cast was dark and gloomy, and pervasive.

"Is *this* it?" Gauguin questioned.

He had expected something greater, something more magical. This was just a puny little body of water with a huge mountain hanging over it. The sullenness of the place depressed him.

Totefa busied himself with wood gathering and did not respond.

Gauguin got down off Ghost Chaser's back. Right away he saw the beautiful rosewood tree, whose roof of leaves touched his head.

"How could I have missed that?" he wondered.

In truth, the tree was enormous. It was like a huge sad, hooded god sitting over the scene—a god of darkness. One thick, knotty limb snaked over the blue-green pool and appeared to drink from the water.

"From this thing, I could carve a marvelous sculpture," Gauguin said. But when Totefa didn't respond, he said loudly, "I must have this limb!"

Totefa stood off a bit and watched. When he heard the first blows of the ax falling recklessly on the giant rosewood branch, it was too late to say anything. He wondered why he had not spoken before.

"Be careful," he cautioned.

But the artist was fully into his work; already he'd taken a big chunk out of the tree limb and exposed its fruity, red wood.

Ghost Chaser whinnied.

Totefa shivered.

The deed was almost done.

While Gauguin raised and swung the famished ax, he composed a poem in his mind:

It is not the tree I am striking
> *But some ghost I cannot see.*
Strike down the forest!
Destroy the ghosts I cannot see!

He felt feverish. "I don't believe in ghosts ... what am I talking about?" he asked himself.

Ghost Chaser whinnied again and stomped his heavy hooves.

The vapors of the bush closed about Gauguin, sealing him in a kind of glistening cocoon. His red beard was doused with droplets. He put his face to the pool and looked at his reflection in the mirror water.

His eyes startled him. They were the orbs of a demon. All red and flushed and wild.

"That isn't me," he mumbled.

Or was it?

Ghost Chaser whinnied a third time. He tossed his mane, flicked his ears, and blew his breath through his nostrils.

Gauguin dropped his ax and sat on the bank of the blue pool. The sweat ran off him in rivulets. He felt hot.

He stood up. One more chop—the branch would break. He struck hard, the drooping limb whined, cracked, and sighed. Then it fell with a crash of glass into the pool.

Totefa, not saying a word, helped Gauguin lug the gnarled limb to the other side of the bank.

"I feel quite warm," Gauguin said. "You feel the same?"

Totefa shook his head. "I don't feel that way."

"I think I am going to have a swim," Gauguin said, taking off his shirt.

Totefa looked apprehensive. "Be careful," he warned.

"Why?" Gauguin said as he waded out into the emerald water. He went in up to his shoulders, and then he swam about, turning circles and rolling on to his back in a frolicsome way.

"It's wonderful." He laughed, splashing wildly. He threw his head back in delight and jetted a spout of water with his mouth.

"Watch out," cautioned Totefa. But he barely raised his voice above a whisper.

Gauguin didn't hear what his friend said.

"I wonder how deep it is?" Gauguin questioned.

Totefa said, "You should come out now."

Gauguin paid him no attention. He dropped like an anchor straight down. Totefa watched the red-haired man sink into the enchanted waters.

Ghost Chaser whinnied for the fourth time.

Gauguin went down, and down.

The pool seems to be bottomless, he thought. The deeper he dropped, the colder the water. He felt he was in a bubble of jade, slowly sinking to the subterranean heart of the earth.

Then something soft, silky, touched his thigh.

At first, he thought it was just some random bit of water weed, or perhaps a small fish. But when he felt it for the second time, he sensed a snakelike, furtive movement. It shied away, returned, encircling him all about his waist, and then retreated once more.

Gauguin shot to the surface, shouting, "Something's in here with me, Totefa."

Totefa said, "I told you to get out of the water!"

Gauguin felt the thing slide against him again. Just a whisper, a furl. A hint of coldness.

Gauguin thrashed violently away from it. And briefly, whatever it was went away—but only briefly.

He heaved vigorously for shore. But the thing came back and wrapped itself around his legs. This time it felt heavy, sodden.

Now Gauguin was only a few feet out from the mossy bank, but when he swam, he was paddle-wheeling to nowhere.

Totefa pushed the rosewood limb toward the floundering

Gauguin, who grabbed it and held on for dear life. As Totefa dragged him out, he felt the thing put out a pulpy, papery tendril all about him.

Gauguin gripped the rosewood branch with white-knuckled desperation.

Then he saw what he would never forget—out of the water, a huge head raised itself . . . a great-eyed beast that blew foam from its nose. The beast was gigantic. It was everywhere, all over him, and he was helpless as it bore down on him.

There is nothing I can do, Gauguin thought, except climb on its back and try to ride it. This he did with surprising skill. As he did so, the envelope of darkness and strangeness, the membrane of the pool that had a hold of him, let go. Gauguin slipped free upon the sand of the little convex shore.

For a moment, he lay there panting. The horrible vision of the beast that had tried to kill him—and then had saved him!— stayed in front of his dazed eyes.

Gauguin blinked. His terror subsided. He was staring into the deep, compassionate eyes of Ghost Chaser. The friendly horse looked curiously at Gauguin and snorted with pleasure.

Totefa laughed.

"What's so funny? I almost drown, and you're laughing!"

"You tried to kill yourself."

"What do you mean?"

"You were fighting—yourself."

Gauguin gasped. "I felt something try to wrap around me and drown me. There's a monster in that pool!"

"You felt Ghost Chaser's tail, you took hold of it, and he pulled you out. That's what happened. I saw it all from here."

Gauguin blinked. There was still an aura of haziness, a phosphorescence that clouded his sight.

Ghost Chaser was munching ferns. His large, wholesome eyes looked calmly in Gauguin's direction. He made a gentle chortle, a little snort, and he bobbed his head from left to right to chase off some flies.

Gauguin got up and walked stiffly over to where Totefa had built a small fire. The cheerful light warmed him. He rubbed his skin.

"I swear—there was something in there," he said, looking back at the blue circlet of water.

Totefa put a stick on the fire.

"Could have been ghosts," Totefa mused. "There are certain spirits that live only in the water. Others live only in trees. Some inhabit the sea, others hang above in the sky. The spirits are everywhere—so we believe."

"Why should a water spirit want to drown me?"

Totefa sat by the fire, his cinnamon skin aglow. His dark eyes shone. He said, "When you cut the tree, you angered the little ghosts of the wood, and when you made so much noise in the pool, you disturbed the quiet ghosts of the springs."

Gauguin felt foolish. What if it were so? What if he were the one who had caused this monstrous thing to happen? What if such ghosts were real?

He was silent for a long time while the wood was eaten by the starving flames. The waterfall sang in a small voice. Ghost Chaser thudded through the thick ferns, grinding his teeth on green stems.

"Totefa?"

"Yes?"

"How do I say I'm sorry to the ghosts of this place?"

Totefa replied with a smile, "You could make a little carving and leave it here."

Gauguin grinned. He could do that, yes, he could.

And he did.

He whittled a rosewood horse, and he set it afloat in the pool of ghosts and left it there.

When he got back to his bamboo house, he carved another horse. This was much larger. He called it *Ghost Chaser,* and he gave it to Totefa as a gift.

No one knows what became of this rosewood ghost horse. But the artist never forgot that spirits dwell everywhere in the Tahitian earth, sky, water, and wind.

Nor did he forget that a horse named Ghost Chaser had saved his life—and he never stopped drawing, painting, and carving horses after that trip to the mountain of ghosts. For, as he often said, "You never have enough good-luck horses around when you live on the enchanted island of Tahiti."

AFTERWORD

The painter who changed the way the twentieth century looked at "primitive art" was changed by his life among the Maori of

Tahiti. He had left Europe in the hope of finding a great adventure with modest means. His desire was to return to a time of human innocence—before war, famine, and what he called "the blight of rationality" had replaced a tribal sense of community and love.

Actually, he did find the place of his dreams. But it wasn't without a certain price. The story of Gauguin's ride into the mountain of ghosts is recorded by the artist himself in his fascinating autobiography, *Noa Noa*. He had many horseback experiences, and we compressed several of them into one. However, the experience of cutting the rosewood limb with Totefa and the strange visions by the pool with his friend are in keeping with the artist's thoughts.

Paul Gauguin's "studio of the tropics," which he planned to share with his on-and-off companion Vincent van Gogh, was both a doorway into heaven and a gateway into hell.

Sadly, the artist suffered from disease, doubt, penury, and painful rejection, and though he believed his little hut was nothing but "space, freedom," sometimes he was plunged into such seasons of despair that some psychologists have labeled him manic-depressive. His feelings of being blinded by darkness and struck dumb by light were very real to him, and they entered into his art at every stroke of the brush.

The classic horse of Tahiti did not come from antiquity, but from recent times. Ghost Chaser came, perhaps, from original stock brought to Tahiti by Captain Cook. Very likely, Cook's equines were Cape ponies (from the Cape of Good Hope) that had Arabian and Thoroughbred blood. They were small and stocky, Dutch-bred animals with the fine heads and facial features of the Arabian. Their faces are as lovable as they are beautiful. So this was a perfect horse to fade into the fastness of the Tahitian wood.

We think Ghost Chaser was a Timor, which had all of the above features. Ghost Chaser looked like a carousel pony, but larger. If you see Paul Gauguin's horse paintings and/or etchings, notice the kindly face, the rounded rump, the lolling grace of Ghost Chaser, whose large-eyed beauty was in keeping with Gauguin's love of innocence.

THE
Karabair

KOURKIG JELALY,
the Horse of the Armenian Highlands

*I*n ancient Armenia, there was a young man whose parents had gone on to the next world. The boy was known simply as David, but one day he would be known as David of Sassoun.

David lived with his aunt and uncle. He was a great horseman; everyone said so. David was the very hero of his household when he picked up his hunting falcon and rode into the meadows to capture quails. One day, though, he came near a field of millet where he was met by an old widow woman in a blue shawl.

"Woe unto your sun," she said in the manner of her people.

David reined his pony and looked at the old woman in her tattered shawl.

"Why do you speak to me so?" he asked.

"You—a young man," she said, scoffing.

"Yes . . . so?"

"Well," she said, rubbing her chin, "what is the son of a great warrior doing hunting sparrows in an old lady's millet field?"

"At least I am doing something."

"Your father had conquered nations when he was your age," she said with a laugh.

"I am not my father," answered David, crossing his leg over his saddle. It made him uncomfortable to hear praises of his dead father. For David had never known him. Actually, David came into the world at the same time his father went out of it. Shortly thereafter his mother died, too, leaving him an orphan.

Now there were only the mysterious tales of his father's heroic deeds and his mother's kindness. David was afraid he'd not measure up to their greatness, and that was why he regarded the old widow with annoyance.

The old woman stared back at him. "Can't you see that it's a pitiful waste of time to hunt birds when those your father once protected, the people of Sassoun, are starving to death? And it is all because of your half brother, Msrah Melik."

"What has his bad blood done now?"

"He has raised the taxes again, so that no one—not even the few and idle rich—can pay. Therefore, all shall starve as one, and that includes you and your horse."

David's falcon shook the hood that covered his head, and

the hawk's bells at his feet rang musically. His pony shook his head, begging to be off upon the hunt.

"My proud bird would tear out the eyes of Msrah Melik," David said, "and I myself would best him in battle, if he ever showed his face here."

It was all talk, of course, but he liked saying it. One thing he knew: his half brother had inherited his father's physical strength and stature, but none of his spiritual grace. In fact, he was a huge cruel person, who served only himself.

"That foolish bird makes you lazy and indolent," she remarked. "You should carry your father's strong bow instead of a hawk."

David grimaced. "Where would I find such a bow? Everyone knows my father's things were buried with him when he died."

The widow shook her head. "Go ask your uncle's wife. She knows where your father's bow is."

It couldn't do any harm. David trotted his pony home and asked his aunt, "Where is my father's bow?"

"David, I would die for you," she said. "But I haven't any idea where that bow is buried."

So, David rode back to the old widow's millet field, and he saw her there, bent under the sun, working. He said, "Old One, my aunt says she doesn't know where it is buried."

The widow spat into her hands and rubbed them together. She kept on with her hoeing and said nothing.

David said, "What shall I do? I have decided you were right. I should help the people of Sassoun and rid them of my cruel half brother . . . but how can I do anything without my father's magic bow?"

"All right," said the old woman, finally paying attention to him. She straightened up and told him that he ought to roast some stones.

"Why should I do that?"

"Because when your aunt sees you roasting stones, she will beg you to come into the house and eat with her. But you will tell her that you are going to eat stones unless she tells you where the bow is hidden."

David rode home forthwith. He did exactly what the widow had told him to do, and this time his aunt relented. She took him into the big, dark barn and showed him where the bow was buried in the deep hay of the loft.

"If you can draw the string of that bow, then it is yours," she said, and stood back while David tried to do it.

Without trouble he bent the bow and fitted the string. His aunt was amazed.

"Is this, then, what I think it is?" she said with a sigh. "The taking of his father's bow and the fulfillment of the legend."

"What legend do you mean?" David asked.

"It is written," she said softly, "that the son of the father would rid the land of his own flesh and blood."

"That would be my half brother, Msrah Melik," said David.

"It is so," said his aunt, and she hung her head in sorrow. For the legend did not say if the son of the father lived afterward, only that he got rid of his half brother. Like everyone else, she hated Msrah Melik, but she feared the loss of her beautiful nephew.

So David practiced with his father's bow every day until he got very good at shooting quail, and he could take a singing sparrow on the wing, too. Soon he became vain over his accomplishment. One day he chanced to ride past the old widow's millet field. He greeted her warmly and showed her his father's bow.

She brushed him and his bow aside, saying, "While you play at war in these fields of childhood, your half brother, Msrah Melik, is murdering your people."

David nodded. "What would you have me do, Old One?"

The widow's words spilled out like a brook.

"Didn't your father ride on a great horse named Kourkig Jelaly?"

David raised and lowered his head. It was true, there had been such a horse. No one had seen him in many years, and David believed he was buried with his father's possessions.

The widow went on, chanting, "Didn't Kourkig have shoes of steel, a bright steel bit, a mother-of-pearl saddle? Didn't Kourkig have golden stirrups on that saddle, and didn't he gallop in the air as well as thunder across the land? And didn't he speak in words that people understand?"

Again David nodded. "They say he did, Old One."

"No," she replied, winking. "You should have said: 'They say he does!'"

"Is Kourkig alive, then?" asked David, surprised.

"Go ask your aunt. And if she doesn't tell you, go roast some more stones."

So, when David returned to his house and saw his uncle forking hay, he begged him to tell the whereabouts of Kourkig. His uncle said, "Ah, David, my dear boy. I would die for you, my son . . . but . . ." Here he paused and looked at the heavens, and then added, "May the mouth draw closed and wither that told you I knew any such thing."

David strode past his uncle, who asked him where he was going.

"I am going to roast stones," he answered, "and I shall eat them until you tell me, or until I die, either way."

His uncle gave in sadly. He, too, had no notion of where all this might end for David, only that Msrah Melik would be driven from the land.

So he showed David where his father's garments and gear were hidden, and where, in the back of the barn, there was a secret stall.

"Therein," said his uncle, "if you remove the bricks, one by one, you shall see the horse of your father."

"How could you feed him if he was walled in?" David wanted to know. His uncle explained that he fed him from a skylight on the roof.

"But remember," said his uncle, "you will not ride Kourkig unless you can draw the saddle girth around his belly."

David answered, "I drew my father's bow, didn't I? And I picked up his armor, too."

"That you did," said his uncle.

"Then I shall draw the girth."

"Watch that he doesn't bite you, David. His jaws are as

strong as a lion's. His hooves will grind you to mush—if he doesn't like you."

David went forth, and with the force of his forearm, he broke through the barricaded wall of the secret stable.

Before him was the world's most beautiful horse.

He was made of mist and quartz. His color was that of a dark ruby. His mane flamed upon his perfectly straight, tall neck. His shoulders quivered with the tension of centuries, and he had all about him a field of energy.

As David entered the sequestered stable, Kourkig drew back in surprise.

Then he began to nicker and prance. David came to him then and took him firmly but gently by the mane. As he traced the outline of Kourkig's eyes with his finger, the great horse smelled his hair and wept.

So David led him out of the darkness of the stable and into the light of the sun. And by the grace of the fire of heaven, the horse began to speak in the manner of a man.

"Earth-born one," he said, "I can see that you are your father's son."

"I am he who has come to ride upon your back."

Kourkig threw back his bronze mane and laughed.

Thus David understood that he was to be tested again.

His uncle, who was standing close by, said, "If you cannot saddle and ride him, he is not yours."

But David lifted the heavy, pearl-studded saddle, and he settled it like a feather on the back of the golden horse.

Kourkig started to rear up to throw it off, but David held

tight to his halter and drew down the horse's lion-colored head. Kourkig sounded an alarm by blowing out his nostrils, the breath of which stunned David for a moment, yet he quickly recovered himself. Then, as swiftly as the falcon's flight, he pulled the girth and fastened it tight. In one smooth motion, he vaulted onto Kourkig's back.

As he did so, sparks shot off Kourkig's hooves, he reared and pawed the air, dropped and kicked up his hind feet. And all the while David stayed in that saddle like a burr, and didn't move.

Then David rode around through the stirred dust of his uncle's barnyard. His uncle watched him go with a wave of his hand. "A thousand woes," he said under his breath, "if the boy is not the man his father was!"

Now it happened that David of Sassoun rode out to fight his crazed half brother, Msrah Melik. He rode as if born to the saddle and the mountains of the north spread out to meet him. He crossed them, one after another, until they faded from behind him and multiplied in front of him.

"How far do we have to go?" David asked Kourkig impatiently.

Kourkig answered, "It is forty days to the last mountain."

David sighed. "Is there no way we can shorten it?"

"I shall change those forty days to forty hours."

"That is still too long."

"Forty hours I shall change to forty minutes."

"That is more than I can wait."

"Forty minutes I shall reduce to forty seconds—look, we are here now."

It was just so. Atop the final mountain, David looked down and saw tents more numerous than the sands in the sea.

He said then to Kourkig, "The stars of the heavens can be counted, but not the tents of Msrah Melik."

"Is that so?"

"Yes. And if those tents were stacks of hay, and I were a raging fire, I couldn't set them afire."

"Is that so?" said Kourkig.

"Yes. And if they were ashes and I were the wind, I couldn't blow them away."

"Ah, my faithless master," said the unweary horse. "Don't waver."

Then Kourkig ordered David to drink from a little stream that sprang up from the rocks, and he obeyed. No sooner had he drunk from the spring than he felt himself calm and refreshed.

"That is the same stream your father drank from when he faced his enemies," Kourkig said.

Suddenly David felt stronger than before. Even his clothes fit him more tightly. His armor was snug; he felt it squeak when he walked.

He mounted Kourkig and went forth into the sea of tents. No soldiers came out to meet him, only one weary old man. It was just before sunup, and no one else was risen.

Now this old man was bareheaded and unarmed, and he said to David, "What are you going to do?"

"I am going to vanquish the enemy," David replied, drawing his sword.

But the old man just shook his head.

"Such words sound good when you say them," he said. "But in truth, they are bad, for, you see, these soldiers have wives and they have children, and if you kill these men, it will weigh heavy on your conscience. Therefore, I must ask you—who is your quarrel with?"

"My quarrel is with Msrah Melik, and no other."

And the old man asked, "For what reason do you have this quarrel?"

"Because he has taxed our people to death and he made slaves of them. Because he burns and loots and kills whenever he is of a mind to do such things."

"Ah, that which you say is bad, but it is also true. You have good reason to fight Msrah Melik."

"Where, then, is he to be found?"

"Do you see that green tent with the golden apple on the top of its tall pole?"

David said he did. The old man said, "Our soldiers will bless you if you kill Msrah Melik, for he is cruel to them, too."

Now it happened that Msrah Melik slept with one eye open. Moreover, he had a pit under his carpet that was forty feet deep and forty feet wide, and it was topped with an iron trapdoor. This pit was designed to house the dead bodies of unwanted visitors. The skinless bones of ravaged prisoners, who died in darkness, were a testament to his cruelty.

David rode up on Kourkig, not knowing any of this, and he called out, "Melik, it is I who have come to fight you. . . ."

Msrah Melik popped his head out of the doorway of the great tent. Seeing his half brother there made him laugh.

"Is it only you, David?" he scoffed.

"I am not afraid of you, Msrah."

"Isn't that nice? I am glad of it—heartened, I might say. So, what would you have me do—clash swords with a boy?"

"I am a boy no more . . . and neither are you a member of our family," David said fairly, and bravely, in his best voice.

"Why don't you come in out of the grace of the sun so that we can talk about your quarrel with me?" said Msrah Melik craftily.

And David, who was, indeed, an innocent person, entered his half brother's tent. Before he could even see Melik's long-twirled mustache, the trapdoor creaked once and gave way with a shudder.

David fell, pell-mell, into the tumbling, cold gloom of the pit.

Wasting no time, Melik laid forty millstones on top of the iron door.

At the same time, Kourkig—seeing all through the open door—turned and galloped off. He went up to the mountain where he and David had first seen the many tents; there he pounded his hooves and caused an earthquake, which cracked open the earth and set David free. Then Kourkig returned. Climbing over the skeletons like a ladder, David got to the upper air, where he met Msrah Melik, who was waiting for him with his lifted mace.

Kourkig saw Melik's weapon rise. Snorting, he made a dust cloud that blinded the evil half brother, so that he staggered and couldn't strike.

David, sword drawn, thrust at Msrah Melik, but his opponent was clever and well trained in swordsmanship. Melik ducked to one side and kicked the sword out of David's hand. Then he again raised his lethal mace and started to bring it down. However, Kourkig advised him not to do it.

"Why not?" asked Melik.

"Because," said the horse, "you are not as strong as you used to be. Furthermore, you haven't had any satisfying sleep. If you strike David a weak blow, surely he will recover and kill you where you stand."

"What would you have me do, horse?"

"You look tired, brother," said Kourkig. "Get sufficient sleep, and we'll come back to you."

Now, Kourkig's words of wisdom made sense to Msrah Melik, who yawned loudly.

"I like to sleep," he said, lowering his mace. "But I love to fight, too. I shall fight David with all my strength—but first, sleep. Meanwhile, since I have spared David, he'll do my bidding while I rest. That is my decree."

"What bidding?" David asked.

"While I sleep and gain back my seven-strengths, you, David, will pull my forty millstones to the top of the mountain. When you are done, wake me, and we will resume our fight."

David accepted his task willingly. So, while Melik snored,

David rolled the heavy millstones to the top of the mountain. But after he had carried only two of them, he was quite exhausted.

"You are too tired to do this," Kourkig told David.

"I shall keep my promise and thus my honor," David replied.

"Yes," spoke the horse, "but I shall help you."

There were, however, forty guards watching their every move to see that David didn't cheat at his task, so Kourkig, as always, did his part in complete secrecy. He stayed at the top of the mountain, and by drawing his breath, he sucked the millstones up the steep hills. David, who seemed to be doing all the work, was actually going through the motions while he slept. Thus did he get as much rest as his adversary.

As the fortieth stone topped the mountain, Msrah Melik awoke.

"I am ready to fight," he cried with much enthusiasm as, once more, he took his position with his mace and David unsheathed his sword.

"Are you tired, David?" asked Melik.

"I am," he answered.

"Well, I must tell you this: I am not tired. And I am prepared to move with such quickness and precision that you won't be able to see what to strike. Shall I show you?"

"Go ahead," David said. "I am ready."

Then Kourkig whispered in David's ear, "He is going to jump swiftly, first to the right and then to the left."

"Which way shall I strike?" David asked too softly for Melik to hear.

And Kourkig answered, "Let your sword make no hesitation, which is what he is counting on. Strike one blow—to the left!"

Melik said, "Well? You said you are ready . . . are you?"

"I am now."

"Good. By the way, David, did I ever tell you that I have wings?"

"You'd better use them."

Then David raised his sword, and it twinkled in the sun. Melik danced to the right, then to the left, moving faster than a hummingbird's heart.

Down the came the sword—*schwah!*

Melik laughed. "You missed! I'm over here! Better strike again, David." He cackled like a crow and his mustache quivered, but David only said, "Msrah Melik, shake yourself."

"Do what?"

"Give yourself a shake."

"Is this some kind of trick?"

Melik shook all over with laughter, and half of his body fell to the right; the other half fell to the left.

And that was how David of Sassoun became the great hero of Armenia. But we know, don't we, that he couldn't have done it without his horse, Kourkig Jelaly, who, they say, is the greatest horse who ever lived in the Armenian highlands.

AFTERWORD

The tale of David of Sassoun and his horse, Kourkig Jelaly, is part of the great oral folk epic of the Armenian people. This story is as old as the Babylonian epic of Gilgamesh. But it has an added distinction. Unlike Gilgamesh, which was written down, the epic of David of Sassoun was recited throughout the centuries, and it was never meant to be preserved as a literary art form. A fragment of it was first transcribed in 1874 in Moush, Armenia.

The story of David of Sassoun was meant to be chanted, and thus it was something to delight people, who sat patiently for hours on end as each new stanza unfolded. The minstrels of medieval times told the tale while carding cotton with a big mallet and a long, bowlike tool. They worked in the light of an open wick lamp fed by flaxseed oil. The wind howled in the chimney. The balladeer sang out his verses and carded his cotton, and everybody left feeling renewed. This kind of telling still existed in the mid-twentieth century in Armenia, and for that matter, it may still exist in some form today.

You may wonder what kind of horse Kourkig was in "real life." Well, it's hard to say, because the tale comes from so long ago. But we imagine Kourkig was a Karabair, one of the oldest and most versatile horses of Central Asia. The Karabair is a small, quick-moving, excellent riding horse with many of the characteristics of the Arabian. This sound and courageous horse is now used to play *kokpar,* Afghanistan's popular form of polo. The origins of the game go back to Genghis Khan, but then, so does the horse.

One fascinating feature of the David of Sassoun myth is that Kourkig speaks to David, advises him, reassures him, and gains for him the stature of a national hero. Some scholars believe this is the first instance in an epic tale where a horse and a man are on an equal footing in the eyes of God. Actually, Kourkig stands taller: he tells David what to do and how to do it, and without him, David never would have defeated his half brother and archenemy, Msrah Melik.

Notes, Sources,
and Acknowledgments

ABJER, THE HORSE OF THE SAHARAN SANDS

We first read of Abjer in *The Romance of Antar* by Eunice Tiet-jens, published by Coward McCann, New York, 1929. Other works that we consulted were *The Horses of the Sahara*, which includes "The Letters of Emir Abd-el-Kader to E. Daumas" (no publisher given), London, 1863. This brought to wonderful life the horsemanship of the Bedouin people. We did further research in *The Arabian Horse in Fact, Fantasy and Fiction*, edited by George H. Conn, A. S. Barnes, New York, 1959.

SNAIL, THE HORSE OF THE AMERICAN PLAINS

Our version of Snail's run was inspired by *Blankets and Moccasins: Plenty Coups and His People, the Crows* by Glendolin Damon Wagner and Dr. William A. Allen, The Caxton Printers, Ltd., Caldwell, Idaho, 1933. We gained further information from *The Mustangs* by J. Frank Dobie, Castle Books, Edison, New Jersey, 1934. Some personal, historical, and anecdotal history of the mustang was supplied by Tesuque, New Mexico, horse wrangler and folksinger Sid Hausman. Thanks are duly given for his insight.

HUMPY, THE HORSE OF THE
RUSSIAN STEPPES

We encountered Humpy in *Little Magic Horse* by Peter Ershoff, translated by Tatiana Balkoff Drowne, Macmillan, New York, 1942. Then, as we were still uncertain of the story's origin, we set out to find another, similar tale and found "The Firebird, Horse of Power, and the Princess Vasilissa," in *Best Loved Tales of the World,* selected by Joanna Cole, Anchor Books, New York, 1982.

In addition, there were still more echoes of Humpy-like characters in the stories translated by Lore Segal in *The Juniper Tree and Other Tales from Grimm,* illustrated by Maurice Sendak, Farrar, Straus & Giroux, New York, 1973. Finally, we discovered *The Tangle-Coated Horse* by Ella Young, Longmans, Green and Co., New York, 1929. In all of these, there is a familiar resonance, so we believe the stories were widely shared around the globe and are part of our common human heritage.

GHOST CHASER, THE HORSE OF THE
TAHITIAN SHADOWS

We had a rare opportunity to view an original early printed work of Paul Gauguin in the midseventies. We had been invited to the Hirschl-Adler Galleries in New York City to see a privately printed edition of the first *Noa Noa*. This rough journal was a reflection of the artist's years in Tahiti from 1891 to 1893. There are only a few of these volumes in existence, and we were looking at one of them in perfect condition.

For a brief moment, while we were holding this little treasure in our hands, it was as if we were seeing through the artist's eyes. This was his original notebook, unedited and roughly drawn, but beautiful in its freshness and strangely primitive style.

For the purposes of writing Ghost Chaser's tale, we studied the commercially printed *Noa Noa: The Tahitian Journal* by Paul Gauguin, translated by O. F. Theis, Dover, New York, 1985. Thanks are due to Norman Hirschl for his kindness.

KOURKIG JELALY, THE HORSE OF THE ARMENIAN HIGHLANDS

This retelling of a portion of the Armenian epic of David of Sassoun was done with an original text close at hand. The translation we used is *David of Sassoun: The Armenian Folk Epic in Four Cycles,* translated by Artin K. Shalian, Ohio University Press, Athens, Ohio, 1964. We had some help as well from the Armenian poet David Kherdian, who took us to the Fresno home of the sculptor Varaz.

At the studio of Varaz we saw the beautiful David riding on the back of his mount, Kourkig Jelaly. The thirty-foot sculpture was something to see. And the story was something to hear, as, of course, Varaz knew the tale and gave us a taste of it while we watched the great horse shimmer in the summer sunlight of the San Joaquin Valley. Kourkig seemed to paw the sky with his huge, bell-sized hooves, and from his bridled lips came the imagined voice of his great wisdom. To David, Veron, Varaz, and the city of Fresno, California, thanks and praises.

About the Art

$\mathcal{W}$hen I was presented with this wonderful manuscript by the Hausmans, I immediately saw the possibilities of creating illustrations in a manner quite different from anything I'd done before. Because the stories come from diverse cultures and time periods, I thought it might be challenging to illustrate the tales in the style of their respective backgrounds. And so I illustrated the story from the old American West in oil on canvas, in the style of Charles Russell and Frederic Remington; the Arabian and Armenian stories (historically very artistically similar) with watercolor and pencil, in the period style of illuminated miniatures; the Tahitian story in oil on canvas, in the style of Gauguin, its subject; and the Mongolian story in gouache on black support, in the style of Russian lacquer boxes. Also, each illustration is bordered with a design reminiscent of the period and culture—the Tahitian paintings, for instance, with a border from one of Gauguin's own designs.

I hope the reader finds as much enjoyment in the variety of characters, locales, colors, and techniques as I found in creating the art for *Horses of Myth*. It was a project of wonderful escapism that took me back to exciting times and places.

—ROBERT FLORCZAK

About the Authors

We link our writing to our lives. We have always been animal people with lots of cats, dogs, horses, shrews, snakes, foxes, wolves, and birds of prey all around us. We have lived in, or very near, a national wilderness area for the past thirty-five years. In New Mexico, we lived between the Tesuque Pueblo and the Santa Fe National Forest. We woke up in the morning hearing horses whinny, and we went to bed at night listening to coyotes wail.

As writers, Loretta and I have been at it quite a while—since the mid-sixties when I published my first book of animal tales based on Navajo myths. One of the stories in that first book, "The Turquoise Horse," became a school text, and it's still in print. We love working together, even though sometimes we squabble over a word, a phrase, and—most often—a fact. Loretta does the research for the books, and she is a real stickler when it comes to facts. I write the stuff down, willy-nilly, and then we collaborate, talking the stories out, as I was taught to do as a storyteller in the Native American tradition. We never write silently but always aloud, each of us saying the phrases until they sound more and more conversational. I usually type on the computer, and while the keys are clicking and we're talking, our Blue-fronted Amazon parrot is yelling right along with us. He thinks he's the real writer in the family. Maybe he is.

For the past ten years we have lived on a Florida Gulf Coast island where there are horses, wild pigs, bobcats, eagles, ospreys, herons, egrets, cormorants, anhingas, manatees, dolphins, and all manner of creepy crawlies. We write with the doors open and the eagles calling. It's a great life, and if we could do it all over again, we'd do it exactly the same way, as writers, readers, listeners, and nature lovers.

—GERALD AND LORETTA HAUSMAN